Ricky the Rookie
Learns Basketball

by
Neha Vashisht

Illustrations by
Mike Motz

To my best friend and biggest supporter, Rajiv, and most importantly, my three crazy boys, Rohan, Rithik aka Ricky, and Revi

Ricky the Rookie Learns Basketball © 2020 Neha Vashisht.
All Rights reserved. No part of this publication may be reproduced or transmitted in any form or by any means, electronic, mechanical, including photocopy, recording, or any information storage and retrieval system, without permission in writing from the author.

Ricky and Rohan are brothers,
but most importantly they are best friends!

They love doing everything together.
They love to play outside at the park, play with their action figures, and even watch movies together.

But there are some things that Ricky doesn't know how to play that Rohan loves doing, especially certain sports.

Ricky tries to play other things like building forts with blocks or drawing fun pictures for his mom, but he always wants to try to learn different sports so he can play with Rohan.

"RoRo, can I play?" Ricky asks.
"But you don't know how to play basketball. That's not even the right ball! That's a soccer ball!" Rohan says, giggling.

Rohan notices Ricky getting sad. "I'm sorry, Ricky. I am just kidding. I will teach you all about basketball," Rohan says as he gives Ricky a big hug.

"Awesome! Thanks, RoRo!" Ricky yells excitedly.
"Now you can teach me, right?"
"Of course. But first, let's call some friends so we can play together!"

Rohan continues to explain.
The only equipment you need in basketball
is an actual basketball and a basketball hoop.

This is the basketball court with a basketball hoop at each end of the court. For a game, there are two teams. Each team has five players on the court at once, and the players try to score as many points as they can by getting the ball into the basketball hoop.

The team with the ball trying to score is on offense. The other team is on defense and is trying to stop the other team from scoring.

Each player has his or her own position. They all have to work together to get the basketball in the basket.

The player with the ball can either pass it to a teammate, dribble it, or shoot it while the other team is playing defense.

If the team with the ball scores a basket, that adds two points to their score, and then the other team has a chance to play offense and make a basket.

The defensive team can try to take the ball away from the offense without touching or hitting the other team's players.

Rohan splits everyone up into two teams, and they start to play.

Rohan's team has the ball first.
They dribble and pass as a team, and shoot, and score a basket!

Next, Ricky's team has the ball. Ricky only dribbles it by himself, but does not pass the ball. Every time he is down the court, someone from the other team steals the ball and scores a basket.

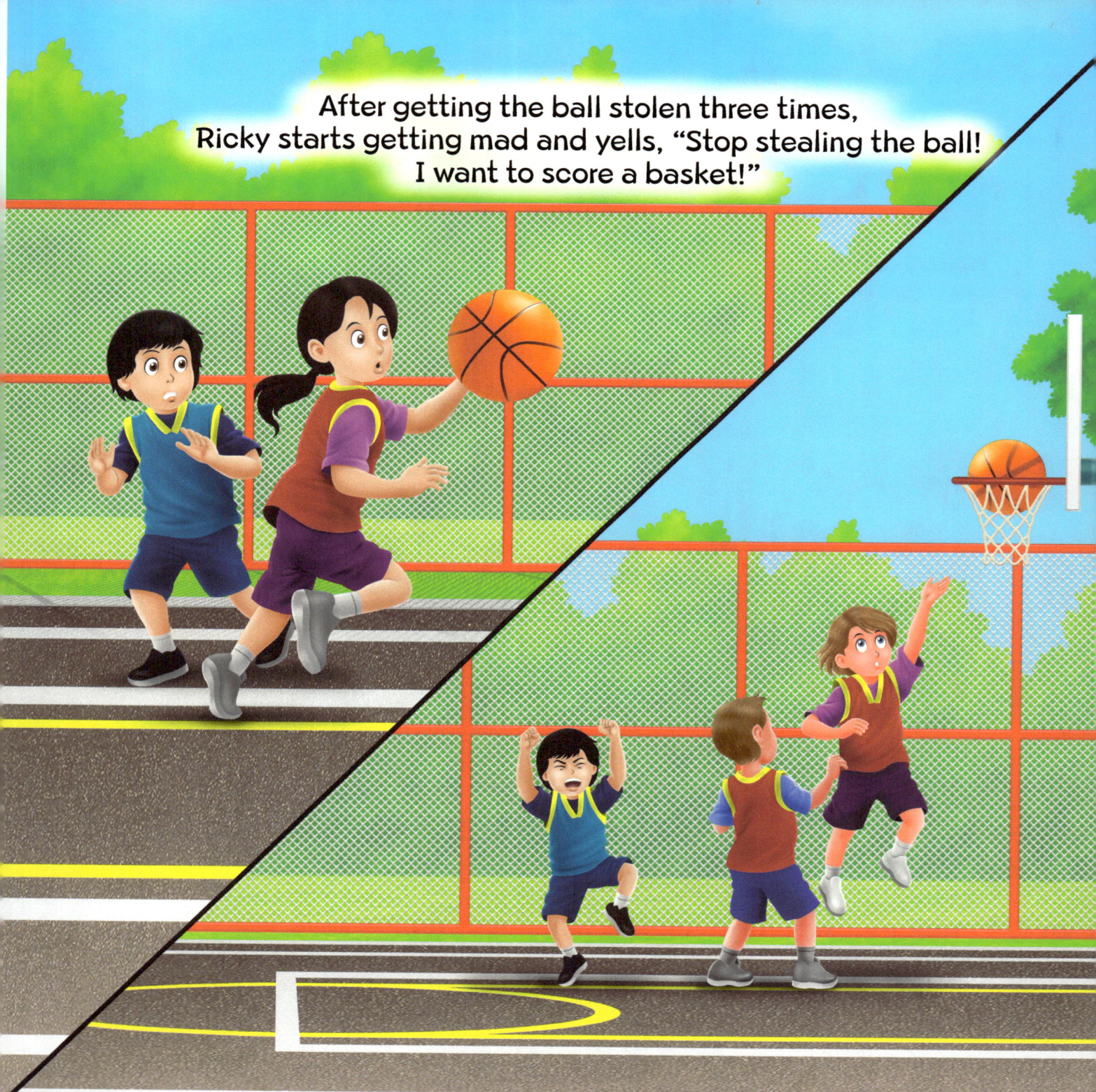
After getting the ball stolen three times, Ricky starts getting mad and yells, "Stop stealing the ball! I want to score a basket!"

"Ricky, it is important to remember that basketball is a team sport. You can't do everything on your own. You also have to pass the ball. One of your teammates may be open and can dribble it and score. If they are being guarded, they can pass it back to you, and you can try to score. But you have to work as a team," Rohan explains.
"Oh, okay. I understand," Ricky exclaims.

"I'm sorry I wasn't passing.
But now I know how to work as a team! Let's play!"

"I knew you could do it!" Rohan says excitedly.
"Thanks for teaching me, RoRo! You're the best big brother!"
Ricky shouts, giving Rohan a big hug.

Meet the Author

Neha Vashisht is a pediatrician who is a busy mom to three young boys. Using books to teach important life lessons and to help through difficult transitions has always been a strong learning tool in her home. As someone who grew up playing multiple sports, Neha wanted to find a way to teach her young children the fundamentals of different sports as well as the important life lessons learned beyond just the physical skills. As she was trying to find books on these topics, she discovered that none were geared towards younger kids. That's how the *Ricky the Rookie* series was born!

In each book, Ricky learns about different sports through the guidance of his older brother, Rohan. Her first book features her favorite sport, basketball, and stresses the importance of teamwork. Neha hopes that through these books, readers will foster a love for learning sports, reading, and sportsmanship.

CPSIA information can be obtained
at www.ICGtesting.com
Printed in the USA
BVHW021400060320
574152BV00001B/1